A Day on the Boat with Captain Betty

written by Diane Murez • *photographs by* Steve Murez

MACMILLAN PUBLISHING COMPANY   NEW YORK

MAXWELL MACMILLAN CANADA   TORONTO

MAXWELL MACMILLAN INTERNATIONAL   NEW YORK   OXFORD   SINGAPORE   SYDNEY

For Selma and Bunky,
with love and thanks

Library of Congress Cataloging-in-Publication
Data. Murez, Diane. A day on the boat with Captain
Betty / written by Diane Murez ; photographs by
Steve Murez. — 1st ed.   p.   cm. Summary:
Two boys take a boat trip around Florida's Sanibel
and Captiva Islands and learn about the area's
wildlife. ISBN 0-02-767430-4   1. Zoology—Florida—Sanibel   Island—Juvenile   literature.
2. Zoology—Florida—Captiva Island—Juvenile
literature. [1. Zoology—Florida—Sanibel Island.
2. Zoology—Florida—Captiva Island. 3. Marine
animals—Florida. 4. Florida—Description and
travel. 5. Boats and boating.]   I. Murez, Steve,
ill. II. Title.   QL169.M79 1993   591.975948—
dc20   92-11428

Sam and Michael woke with the birds in the faint sun glow before dawn. They were going island hopping with Captain Betty. She had told them they would discover marvelous shells and sea creatures.

Captain Betty was waiting for them at the dock. "Welcome aboard *Piece-a-Cake,*" she said, smiling. She helped the boys stow their gear and put on life preservers.

Sam noticed a bucket full of wriggling shrimp. Captain Betty put one into his hand and he laughed. "It tickles. It's squirmy!"

"Yes, but shrimp are good bait if we decide to do a little fishing," Captain Betty said. "Local fish like snook, mangrove snappers, and redfish prefer live bait, especially shrimp."

Sam and Michael could hardly wait. Waving good-bye to their parents, they were off! The wind tugged at their faces and hair. The sun sparkled on the boat's wake.

Captain Betty cruised easily through a maze of big and little islands.

"How do you know where to go?" "Why are there so many little islands around here?" Michael and Sam asked at the same time.

Captain Betty laughed. "Hold on a minute with those questions. I can't answer everything at once. I have a map, but mainly I'm just familiar with these waters. At first, I used to take my boat out exploring, going out a little bit farther each time. I got to know the birds, shells, and wildlife on each island and where the water was shallow. Sometimes I ran aground on a sandbar and had to climb out and tug the boat with a rope, but I only got stuck on each sandbar once. After that I always remembered where they were…．

"To answer your other question, look over there," Captain Betty said, pointing to a tiny piece of land with a single tree on it. "Most of the islands around here begin as sandbars—piles of sand left by the wind and currents.

Eventually they become real islands when mangrove trees, like the one you see, start to grow."

"How does that work?" Sam asked, not sure that he understood how a tree could turn a sandbar into an island.

"Well, the red mangrove is a unique kind of tree," answered Captain Betty. "Its seeds can stay alive in saltwater for a long time. Sometimes the seeds float hundreds of miles. When they bump into some warm, sunny sand they stop and put down roots. Those roots are very special, too. They are covered with a skin that keeps out salt, so the tiny seedling (and later the tree) can survive in saltwater. They're called 'prop roots' because they help prop up the mangrove. As the tree grows, the prop roots collect more sand, fallen leaves from the tree, seashells, and other things. Gradually the land is built up and provides food and a home for other living creatures."

Soon Captain Betty stopped the boat at an island the size of a large house. Herons, cormorants, egrets, and

pelicans were perched everywhere. They were calling and crying and squawking in an amazing concert.

Despite all the noise, Captain Betty motioned to the boys to be quiet. "If *we* make a commotion, the birds might fly away. Or the babies might get excited and fall out of their nests—and their parents won't pick them up."

The boys sat very still and listened as Captain Betty explained in a quiet voice, "Birds only come to this island in April, May, June, and sometimes July, depending on the weather. They come here to hatch their eggs safely. Cormorants, brown pelicans, great blue herons, cattle egrets, great egrets, and snowy egrets all nest at the same time, always returning to the same rookery island."

A great brown pelican swooped down to the branch where three bald, screaming baby birds were waiting. The tiny pelicans scrambled to their mother's throat pouch to eat the fish she had caught, partially digested, and spit back up for them.

"Those are brown pelicans, now an endangered species," Captain Betty whispered. "Pesticide almost made them disappear in the 1970s. Pelicans' eggshells became so fragile that they broke when the mother sat on them. Since DDT was banned in 1972, the shells are stronger now. Look at their nest—that big ball of sticks. It has to be really strong, because the babies grow in it for about twelve weeks. They're born completely naked and don't even have any down for the first two weeks. As they grow, their appetites become enormous. Their parents have to go fishing four or five times a day to feed them. After a while, the young birds start fighting for the fish they scoop out of their parents' gullets. They hit one another over the head with their wings. Only the strongest get enough food to live."

Captain Betty let the boat drift away, gently, so as not to frighten the birds.

"Now keep a lookout for osprey nests," Captain Betty told the boys. "Ospreys like to build way up high—fifteen

to fifty feet—mostly in tall trees, but they can also make do with telephone poles. Out here on the water they use channel-marker posts. You can't miss an osprey nest—it's enormous. Ospreys always return to the same nest, adding to it year after year, sometimes for as long as forty years. They like to decorate their nests with junk collections. People have found towels, seashells, jewelry, dolls, and even brooms. Once the nest is nice and cozy, both parents take turns sitting on the eggs, caring and fishing for their babies."

Suddenly Michael shouted, "I see one! I see a nest with a whole family in it!"

As *Piece-a-Cake* approached, the big osprey screeched and glared, flapping its wings furiously, to scare them away from the baby birds. Just then another adult osprey came flying back to the nest clutching a fish in its claws.

"Look how the osprey carries the fish, head into the wind, to cut down wind resistance. Ospreys know almost everything about catching fish, since that's all they eat. In fact, the osprey's nickname is 'fishhawk.' They can swoop down from one hundred fifty feet. They always fish alone, plunging down feet first to grab the fish in their claws. Ospreys have two claws in front and two in back, with barbs to hold the slippery fish. Besides being great fishermen, ospreys are very well mannered. After eating, they always wash their claws."

"I think they look like eagles," Sam said.

"Ospreys and eagles are both birds of prey, ones that kill and eat other animals, and they do look enough alike for people to confuse them," replied Captain Betty. "The easiest way to recognize an osprey is by its white breast feathers; the eagle's are dark. The osprey is also much smaller and has a dark band across its face."

Soon they arrived at the next island. The boys waded ashore onto a long, dazzling beach covered with thousands of seashells. Michael started heaping up shells all around his brother.

"Sam, you look like a Calusa shell mound," said the Captain.

"What's that?" asked Sam.

"The Calusas were a powerful, ancient seafaring tribe who were living here long before Columbus. They built shell mounds that are scattered all over these islands. Some of the mounds were garbage dumps, some were watchtowers, and some were temples for religious dances and sacrifices. They also used shells and fish bones to make weapons, utensils, masks, and jewelry. We don't really know what happened to the Calusas. Only their shell mounds remain."

Captain Betty gave each boy a net bag. "Let's look for some seashells," she said. "Every shell is unique, just like a fingerprint."

Sam and Michael looked at her in surprise. Most of the shells looked pretty much the same to them.

Captain Betty added, "Not only that, but looking for shells is different each time, because the tides and weather constantly change the beaches. It's always surprising to see what nature has put there for you."

Captain Betty waded into the water, stopping at the surf zone, where the waves break. The boys joined her. Michael quickly held up his first find.

"That's a pen shell," said Captain Betty. "Pens are the guardians of the shell world. They dig their pointed ends into the sand under the water, and anchor themselves there with a bunch of threads called a byssus. During storms, large groups of pens act as fences to keep other shells from being washed ashore, where they would die."

"Why can't they live out of water?" asked Michael.

"Mollusks, as scientists call this type of animal, can't

Above clockwise from left: tulip shell, worm shells, horseshoe crab, lightning whelk and egg case, lightning whelk

Facing page clockwise from top middle: baby's ear, Sunray Venus clam, murex, pen shell

take oxygen directly from the air. Their bodies are only able to get food or oxygen from water. Of course, they can manage for several hours on the beach by digging in and waiting for the next tide. Some, like coquinas, even live in wet sand. But no mollusk can survive very long in dry sand."

As Sam and Michael continued looking, the shells, which had seemed so much the same at first, took on their own names and personalities. The boys found a baby's ear, some tulips, a Sunray Venus clam, a murex, two worm shells, and even the remains of a horseshoe crab.

Then Sam discovered what he thought was a sea serpent. He rushed over to Captain Betty, who opened it up. There were tiny shells inside. "This is a lightning-whelk egg case," said Captain Betty. "The female whelk attaches one end of this case to a rock or buries it in the sand with anywhere from twenty to one hundred whelks inside. The baby whelks start eating each other as soon as they hatch, so only the strongest grow up. And do they grow! Along with horse conches, lightning whelks are the biggest shells you'll find in these parts. They get their name from the streaks on them that look like lightning bolts, but they remind me the most of grandparents. They get whiter as they get older. In fact, some of the very old ones are pure white. With or without the 'lightning' marks, you can always identify them: Lightning whelks are the only shells with spirals curving to the left. The Calusas used them for hammers, picks, cups, and ladles."

Concentrating on their shelling, the boys almost bumped into
a flock of ibis. The ibis were stirring up the sand with their long,
downward-curving bills to find insects and shellfish. As Sam and
Michael approached, two of the birds broke away, soaring into
the brilliant blue sky. Captain Betty told the boys that the ancient
Egyptians considered the ibis sacred. They believed the god
Thoth always came to earth as an ibis. "It certainly wasn't sacred
in America," she said. "The Indians and early settlers killed ibis
and ate them like turkeys. Luckily, they're protected by conser-
vation laws now."

"I'm glad!" said Sam. "They're beautiful."

"I think so, too, especially this season," said the Captain. "This
is when they breed, so their legs and bills are bright red instead
of pink. When they're ready to nest, large groups of them will
gather together on a rookery island for about two weeks. Then,
suddenly, all the ibis will start flapping their wings and flying back
and forth like crazy. After they've flapped all the leaves off the
trees, they'll settle down and build their nests."

"Pretty weird," said Michael. "Pretty birds, but weird."

Captain Betty, who had continued shelling, called out, "Here's a shark's eye!"

"A real one?" asked Sam.

"No, that's only the name for this shell. It's also called a cat's eye or a moon snail. If you look at it closely, you can see a little hole where another mollusk bored through it to eat the soft flesh inside."

"Eat it? That's disgusting," said Michael.

"Well, just as people love to eat oysters, crabs, and clams," replied Captain Betty, "some mollusks eat each other. This shark's eye probably ate lots of coquinas, for instance. Other carnivorous mollusks have various hunting techniques. Some drill holes in other shells with a pointed, spearlike body part called a radula. Others pry or wedge their dinner open. Some mollusks stun their prey with muscle-relaxing chemicals. The real killer mollusks are the cones, who stab their victims with radulae that have poisonous teeth on them. American cones are not dangerous, but some in the South Pacific have a truly deadly poison."

Michael was just beginning to picture gigantic seashell battles when Sam shouted, "Look! This one's alive!"

"That's a Florida fighting conch. Put it on the sand and watch." Very slowly the conch somersaulted away from them down the beach.

"Wow!" said Michael, hardly able to believe he was watching a walking seashell. "Can it really fight?"

"No," laughed Captain Betty. "It's pretty spunky, though. Most mollusks just pull back into their shell and draw up their operculum—a hard part on the end of their foot—like a door and shut up tight. The fighting conch will thrash around a bit and try to beat a retreat by pushing with its foot, as you just saw. It's actually a peaceable kind of shell, eating mostly algae and keeping out of the way of hungry, meat-eating mollusks. I've been told that it was named 'fighting' because its points reminded people of the spikes worn by Roman gladiators. Actually, the fighting conch is so friendly that it often shares its shell with little crabs."

Michael was disappointed that the fighting conch didn't really fight, but he cheered up when he found a live clam. He wasn't at all sure that it looked like a good thing for a human being to eat.

"Lunchtime," announced Captain Betty. "All aboard."

Before they lifted anchor, Captain Betty said, "Many people don't realize that live shells are animals that need to reproduce. If people keep taking them, we won't have enough shells some day." The boys carefully searched through their buckets to rescue any live shells. Before throwing the last one back into the sea, Sam kissed it good-bye.

Captain Betty turned to him with a twinkle in her eye. "How would you like to steer *Piece-a-Cake*?"

Sam's face burst into happiness. He listened carefully to Captain Betty's instructions, then took the helm.

Sky and sea streamed past him. Water sprayed his face. The boat bumped, but he held on and kept it straight. He felt proud to be a captain, even if only for a little while.

Captain Betty maneuvered the boat into the dock and Sam and Michael helped to tie it up. During lunch, Sam asked a lot of questions about going to "sea school," and getting a Coast Guard license. Captain Betty told him about learning "the rules of the nautical road" and seamanship. She explained how navigation lights work at night and how flags are used for signaling in the daytime. "For instance, flying a flag of three black balls in the rigging means, 'I am aground.'" She said that a captain also had to know about knots, anchoring, weather, and first aid in case of an emergency on board. The boys thought it sounded like a lot to learn, but both agreed they would like to become captains some day.

Leaving the cove after lunch, Captain Betty shouted, "Look to starboard! A manatee!"

Michael and Sam turned quickly. A funny looking brown muzzle was peeping out of the water. Captain Betty turned off the motor. The boys saw the creature roll over and throw something into its mouth with its flipper, just like a person eating popcorn.

"What is that?" Michael wanted to know.

"Manatees are mammals—distant relatives of elephants—that live in the water," explained the Captain. "Some people call them sea cows because they spend most of their time in herds, munching on sea grasses. We're lucky to spot them—it doesn't happen every day. There used to be huge herds of them roaming up and down the southeastern coast. Christopher Columbus even mentioned manatees in his ship's log. But now there are only a thousand or so left in the United States, mainly in Florida."

"What happened to them all?" asked Sam, upset.

"Well, the manatee is very gentle, very slow. It has trouble escaping from its enemies—sharks, alligators…and people. People used to hunt manatees, and have killed many in boating accidents. Since they only have one baby every three years or so, manatees are disappearing faster than they can multiply. Naturalists predict that in thirty years we won't be seeing any more of them."

Captain Betty sighed. "It's really a shame. They're such affectionate, fun-loving animals. They nuzzle and hug each other with their flippers."

Just then a baby manatee rode by on its mother's back. "The young stay close to their mothers, nursing for about two years," Captain Betty said. "And they give a special,

high-pitched call if they get lost. In fact, manatees act so much like humans sometimes, that legends of mermaids probably started when sailors saw manatees playing from far away and thought they were sea people."

The boys watched the manatees until the animals' shapes blended into the shifting light and shadows of the water. The boat rocked in the hot afternoon sun. Michael began to feel drowsy. He gazed at the watery waves…

...and saw a house float by. He thought he must be dreaming until Captain Betty said, "I wonder who's moving?"

"That's someone moving?" Sam exclaimed, surprised.

"Yes, towing their house is the easiest way for people who live on a small island to move," said Captain Betty, matter-of-factly. "Instead of having to transport all the building materials for a new house, they just float the old one, with all its pots and pans inside, to the new location."

After seeing so much that was new and different, both boys felt tired. They curled up under towels and went straight to sleep.

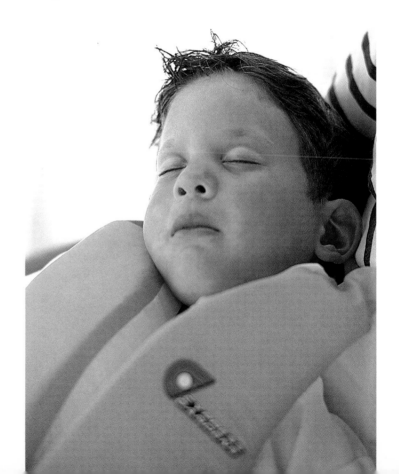

When they awoke, they saw clear turquoise water lapping onto a deserted shoal. "This is a good place to find sand dollars," said Captain Betty. "Sand dollars tend to choose beds that have the food they eat. They burrow into the sand, but in clear, shallow water like this, you can see their special pattern—shaped like the spokes of a wheel. By the way, you might also find some shark's teeth."

Michael and Sam gave great yells, jumped down from the boat, and started looking. Almost at once they dug up several sand dollars. The live ones were brown and hairy and left a yellow stain on their hands, which the Captain said could be used for dyeing fabric. Michael chose a dead sand dollar because it was bright white, and put it in a little cockleshell boat with his other favorites.

Sam still longed to find a real shark's tooth. Captain Betty explained that teeth were the only really hard part of a shark's skeleton and didn't rot. She said, "Every time a shark takes a hearty bite, which they can do with a force of three thousand pounds per square inch, they lose two or three teeth in the process. New ones move forward to replace them. So, a good-sized shark can make up to twenty thousand teeth in a lifetime."

With that number of teeth being lost, Sam considered that he had a good chance of finding at least one. He put on his mask and fins to search along the shoal, and finally he found one! Michael stuck the tooth in his mouth, pretending he was a shark. They all laughed and laughed.

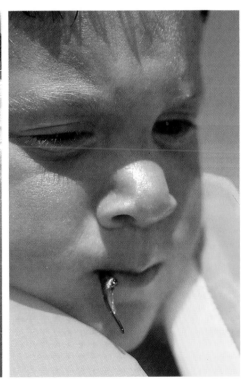

Then Sam and Michael ran along the beach, dipping and kicking and splashing. They swam underwater and made faces at each other.

"You two look like a couple of manatees," Captain Betty laughed.

All of a sudden, Michael ran up out of the water. "What about going fishing?" he wanted to know.

"Let's go!" said Captain Betty. She took the boat to a narrow channel between two islands, where the water was dark green and still. The air was full of whirring sounds and mysterious animal cries. It reminded Michael of a jungle—a little bit scary.

While they waited for the fish to bite, Captain Betty told pirate stories. "In the 1700s and 1800s, Florida's West Coast, with all its islands and deep mangrove forests, used to be the perfect hideout for thieves and pirates. The most famous were a bloodthirsty pirate captain Gasparilla, his sidekick Black Caesar, and their buccaneers. They roamed the area, looting and taking captives. As the story goes, Gasparilla fell in love with a Spanish princess he had captured. When she wouldn't marry him, or give him her hand, as they said in those days, he chopped it off. Lots of old-timers swear that pirate treasure is still buried all over these islands."

Sam was thrilled. He left his fishing and, imagining he was a pirate, climbed up a mangrove tree next to the boat. "I'm going to scout around for some gold," he swaggered. But all he could see were trees, birds, and logs floating in a greenish lagoon.

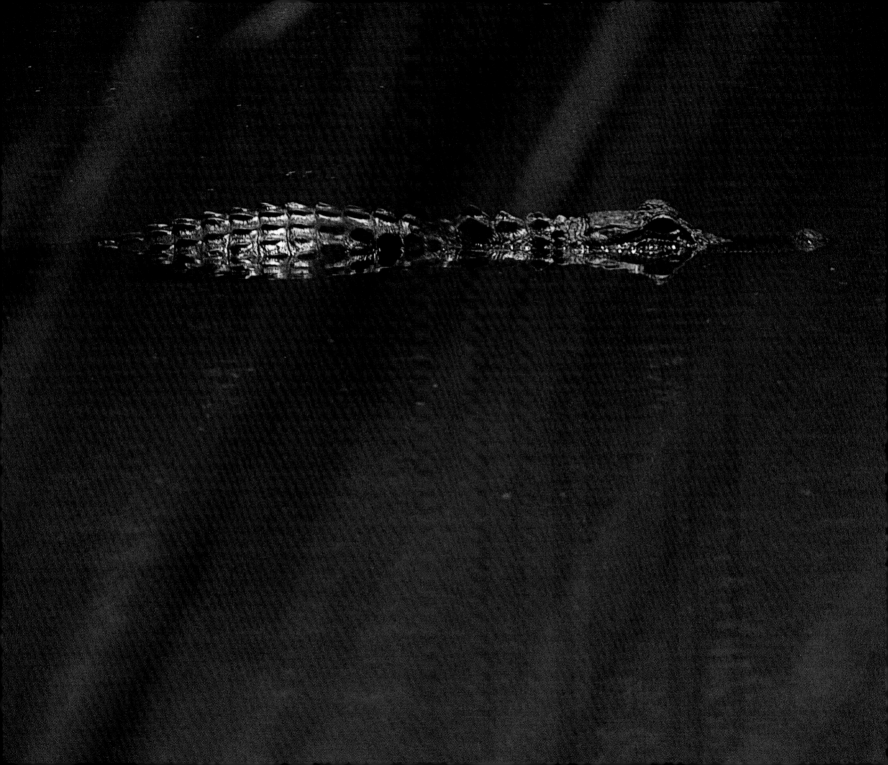

Suddenly one of the logs blinked. It was an alligator! Sam forgot all about being a pirate. He scampered down the tree and back into *Piece-a-Cake*.

"There's an alligator guarding the gold!" Sam cried. "Let's get out of here."

Sam shuddered, but Captain Betty said quickly, "I bet you didn't know that alligators play an important role in saving other animals." Sam and Michael looked doubtful. Captain Betty went on. "During droughts alligators dig deep into the grass and mud, using their tails, feet, and mouths until they reach fresh water. They make these gator holes to keep their skins from drying out, which would be fatal for them. At the same time, gator holes rescue other birds and animals who would otherwise die of thirst.

"You still don't look enthusiastic, but I'll have you know that the American alligator is the most gentle of the world's alligators. It won't attack people unless provoked. That doesn't mean it's not dangerous. A full-grown alligator can run as fast as a human being and a mother alligator may get ferocious defending her nest. But in general, if you don't bother them they won't bother you. The only real exception is an alligator who's used to being fed. They lose their fear of man and will approach human beings. But if you don't feed an alligator or bother one who's guarding a nest, alligators are pretty safe and interesting to watch."

Sam still looked a little shaken, so Captain Betty said, "I have an idea." She attached a kite to one of the fishing rods. As they zoomed along, the kite leaped and danced in the wind. "This is much better than fishing," Michael said happily.

Both Sam and Michael agreed that it had been a most wonderful day. They thanked Captain Betty warmly. Full of good feelings inside, the three of them watched a last flock of ibis fly by as the sun set, and *Piece-a-Cake* headed home.